The Legend of the Two Moons

Written and Illustrated by Francisco X. Mora

Highsmith
P R E S S

Fort Atkinson, Wisconsin

Published by Highsmith Press
W5527 Highway 106
P.O. Box 800
Fort Atkinson, Wisconsin 53538-0800

The paper used in this publication meets the minimum requirements of American National Standard for Information Science - Permanence of Paper for Printed Library Material. ANSI/NISO Z39.48-1984

About the Author

Francisco Mora was born in Mexico City in 1952, where he studied traditional and contemporary art with some of Mexico's most influential artists. Later he continued his studies in Europe and the United States. With bright colors, mythical creatures and Mexican folklore, he creates a whimsical world of fantasy that subtly teaches about reality. His writing and illustrations are interpretations of his dreams, memories and past, which draw heavily on his childhood recollections of the sights, sounds and flavor of his Mexican heritage.

Library of Congress Cataloging-in-Publication Data

Mora, Francisco X.
    The legend of the two moons / written and illustrated by Francisco
X. Mora.

        p.   cm.
    Summary: A tale which explains how there came to be only one moon
in the night sky.
    ISBN 0-917846-15-X (alk. paper) : $19.00
    [1. Folklore --Mexico. 2. Moon --Folklore.] I. Title II. Title:
Legend of the 2 moons.
PZ8. 1 .M79Le 1992
398.26--dc20
[E]   92-31552
                                                CIP
                                                 AC

It was night, and all the animals of *la selva* had found a place to sleep.

Only *Chucho* the dog was still looking for a warm bed.

Singing as he went, he wandered along the moonlit dirt path, down by the big pond of water, called *el cenote*.

As he passed under the *tamarindo* tree, he heard a deep voice say, "Who is making all that noise down there?"

"It's just me, *Chucho*, Felipe's dog."

The deep voice from up in the tree inquired again, curiously. "What are you doing here? It's almost night and *los animalitos* of the jungle have already gone to sleep."

"I am looking for a quiet place to sleep. Felipe and his family are having a *fiesta*. They have been singing and dancing all evening."

Suddenly, a little green parrot flew down from the tree top.

"Don't be afraid, *Chucho*. I'm the voice you heard in the tree. *Me llamo Perico.* Sometimes I pretend to have a very deep voice to scare away unwelcome visitors."

"You seem like a nice dog. Why don't you sleep in my tree tonight?"

Chucho accepted the parrot's invitation and climbed up into *el árbol*. With some leaves and twigs, *Chucho* made his bed in the highest branches of the tree.

As he arranged his bed, he tried to pull some bigger branches closer to keep him warm.

Uno. Dos. Y tres. Three times he tried to pull the branches closer but with no luck. Each time they sprang back. *Uno. Dos. Y tres.* He pulled again without success.

Just as he was going to give up, *Chucho* saw the moon shining brightly through the branches.

"The light of *la luna* is so bright!" he exclaimed.

"Naturally, the moon is bright. You are much closer to the moon up here in the tree top," replied *Perico*.

Pushing the branches apart to get a better look at the moon, *Chucho* suddenly cried out with great surprise.

"I cannot believe my *ojos*. Not only is the moon so bright, there are TWO moons!" exclaimed *Chucho*.

Chucho had never known there to be two moons!

"How beautiful they are."

The parrot looked for himself to see if *Chucho* was telling the truth.

"*¡Es verdad, Chucho!* There are two moons! I must be dreaming, but I am not asleep!" said the parrot.

"*Mi abuela* used to tell stories of two moons, but I thought that was just a legend," said *Chucho*.

"I know why we have never noticed the two moons before. They only appear at a certain time of the year. That must be the reason!" *Perico* guessed.

"These moons are so special that we must capture one for ourselves. Then when the nights are dark, *la luz* from our moon will shine into our beds and we will not be afraid."

"But the two moons are beautiful together as they are in the sky. Let's leave them both so that we can enjoy looking at them," *Chucho* replied.

"No, we must capture one moon and keep it. If you won't help me, I will do it myself."

With that, *Perico* jumped from the branches and flew away.

From the tree top, *Chucho* watched as *Perico* flew
swiftly toward the two moons.

Perico pulled with all of his might, trying to capture the moon. But the moon seemed fixed in place. *Perico* pushed the moon with all of his strength, but still it would not move. *Perico* gave one last shove and *¡zas!* the moon came loose!

Perico grabbed the moon in his beak and flew back towards the *tamarindo* tree.

Chucho watched *Perico* flying in circles above him, carrying the moon in his beak.

But the moon was too heavy for *Perico* to carry all the way to the *tamarindo* tree.

With a huge splash, the parrot and the moon fell into *el cenote*.

Chucho ran to *el cenote* where he found the wet
parrot crying.

"My moon, my moon. I have lost it forever," sobbed
Perico.

"You should not have been so greedy as to want the
moon for yourself," *Chucho* scolded the parrot.

As *el agua* became calm again, *Perico* saw something glowing at the bottom of the pool.

"Look, there is our moon!" he exclaimed, pointing to the water.

And to the surprise of *Chucho* and *Perico*, the moon was there, glistening under the water.

Chucho and *Perico* climbed back into their beds.
They felt safe even in the darkness of *la noche*
because *la luna* in *el cenote* was shining so brightly.

They were also very happy because they again had two moons. One moon glows brightly in the sky. And the other moon, the one the parrot lost that night, glows from under the water at the bottom of *el cenote*.

Glossary of Spanish Words

los animalitos	the little animals	*los ojos*	the eyes
el aqua	the water	*la selva*	the jungle
el árbol	the tree	*el tamarindo*	tropical fruit tree of Mexico
el cenote	the pool of water		
Chucho	Dog (common Mexican term)	*Uno. Dos. Y tres.*	One. Two. And three
la fiesta	the party	*¡Es verdad!*	You tell the truth!
la luna	the moon	*¡zas!*	bang!, loud sudden noise
la luz	the light		
Me llamo Perico	My name is Perico		
Mi abuela	My grandmother		
la noche	the night		
Perico	Parrot		